T0105813

# It's Lonley at the Bottom

Jimmy Carter

*We at Trafford believe that it is the responsibility of us all, as both individuals and corporations, to make choices that are environmentally and socially sound. You, in turn, are supporting this responsible conduct each time you purchase a Trafford book, or make use of our publishing services. To find out how you are helping, please visit www.trafford.com/responsiblepublishing.html*

*Our mission is to efficiently provide the world's finest, most comprehensive book publishing service, enabling every author to experience success. To find out how to publish your book, your way, and have it available worldwide, visit us online at www.trafford.com*

*Trafford rev. 12/03/2009*

 www.trafford.com

**North America & international**
toll-free: 1 888 232 4444 (USA & Canada)
phone: 250 383 6864 ♦ fax: 250 383 6804 ♦ email: info@trafford.com

**The United Kingdom & Europe**
phone: +44 (0)1865 487 395 ♦ local rate: 0845 230 9601
facsimile: +44 (0)1865 481 507 ♦ email: info.uk@trafford.com

# CHAPTER 1

It was a typical Monday morning at the office. Everyone was sitting idly around with a scowl on their faces. When one of the bosses walked by, everyone would hover over their desks, reminiscent of the Industrial Revolution.

I work at a Government Aircraft Repair Facility. I have worked here for ten years. During that time, I have learned that education, knowledge of the job and diligent work are not the keys to success at this facility. I have never been promoted, received a monetary reward, a commendation or even a "Good Work" for doing all the work for the heros of this organization.

My name is Bartholomew Stinson, everyone calls me Bart. I am an equipment Specialist. My immediate supervisor is Neb Foulcar. Neb is about five feet eight inches tall and has a dark complexion, squinty eyes and large ears. Neb is infamous throughout the facility for being extremely caustic and obnoxious, but the only ones he irritates are the people that he comes into contact with. The Office Manager is Bid Brashear, a balding man in his late sixty's, with sagging jaws, he gained his position simply through longevity, he has been with the government for forty-six years, a man who should be retired. The Projects Manager is Zeke Humbolt, Zeke is tall with black hair and a aquiline nose, he has squinty black eyes and never manages to look a person in the eye, a man that I would not buy a used car from. Zeke gained his position by playing ball with the "Good Ole Boys" of the organization.

I arrived at the repair facility ten years ago full of ambition, hope and the desire to do a sterling job on everything that I did. I was greeted by a secretary named Karen Lindlow, who was wearing a light blue pant suit, which went well with her silver hair. Karen was a handsome woman, about fifty years old and a little on the hefty side, who had been with the government for a long time. She was smiling and friendly and seemed to have a cheerful disposition, but as the day wore on, I began to sense that her cheerfulness was a forced façade.

She took me to Bid Brashear's office and we were introduced. He was about six feet tall with a hair line that had almost finished receding. He was in his sixties with bags under his eyes and drooping cheeks. I was told that he was a benevolent fellow who invited all the female visitors to the facility to stay at his place and save their motel money. He welcomed me to the office and he told me, "If you need anything, let him know", an exercise in insincerity. We then left and Karen introduced me to the other employees in the office. They were cordial, but I sensed that they were not really very happy with their positions. We then left the office and went to other departments in the facility. I was introduced to the Project Manager of Logistics. His Name was William Sturges, he was a distinguished looking man with shades of gray beginning to color the hair on his temples. He told me, "Welcome to Disneyland North." I thought that that was a strange thing to say to a new employee, but he seemed to be a fairly intelligent man. I was soon to learn that fairly intelligent people were not popular here. After touring the facility, we returned to the office where I would toil for the next ten years..

# CHAPTER 2

On Wednesday of the third week that I was there, everyone was working at their desks with their usual demeanor. The humdrum atmosphere was suddenly broken. One of my fellow coworkers named Leon Cambell came to Neb's desk. Leon is a highly nervous and easily excitable individual, he has very thin eyebrows and sandy hair that looks like it belongs on a rooster, Leon does not take interruptions to his work or criticism very well. Leon said, "Go ahead, do it." Neb said, "Do what?" Leon shouted, "Screw me" Neb replied, "What are you talking about?" Leon shouted again, "Screw me, I know that you are going to do it before the day is over, so go ahead and do it, I can't stand the suspense!" Since all this was in easy earshot of everyone in the immediate area, giggles began to emanate throughout the office. Leon left Neb's desk and walked to the center of the room and said, "I don't think this is very funny." Leon then stomped out of the office and slammed the door.

I was then called to Bid Brashear's office because, for the fourth time, Neb had been to Bid's office to complain about me. I had to wait awhile before I could see Bid because our office secretary had been promoted and Bid was interviewing a lady who had applied for the job. He took one look at her headlights and said, "You are hired". When the applicant, whose name was Sharon Wilson and was a very attractive woman left, I knocked on Bid's door and was told to come in. Bid told me to' "Take a seat and that he wanted to talk to me." He started off talking cordially about how we were all a team and should be able to get along with each other.

Before the discussion could go any further, another coworker came into Bid's office. It was Wendy Ryan. Wendy is another worker who has been with the government for a long time. She is pretty smart and capable but is never selected for promotions. She is a little on the heavy side with prominent worry lines extending from her eyes, which are amplified by the fullness of her cheeks. She is a stickler for following the book; so much that she has the tendency to get on peoples nerves for trying to follow all rules, whether they apply to the current situation or not.

Wendy told Bid that," she wanted to talk to him about the way we were handling transitions from shelf to production lines." Neb told her that," we were doing it the way that I want to do it." Wendy said, "But Bid it is against regulations." "Fuck the regulations!" Bid answered. Wendy said, "But the specification says--." Bid interrupted, "Fuck the specification, now go on back to your desk and quit bothering me." Wendy replied, "But Bid"; Bid interrupted her again, "I told you to go on back to your desk, now go on!" Wendy left the office with tears streaming down her face. Bid told me," You go on too, and try to get along with Neb."

When I left Bid's office, he followed me back to our unit. He told Neb that," He wanted to talk to him. He took Neb to an empty desk, but it was in hearing distance of everyone in the immediate area. He told Neb that "He wanted a full audit on every piece of equipment on the A12 Production Line." Neb told him "Yes sir, I will get someone on it immediately." Bid told him "No, this is very important, I want you to do the audit personally!" "Yes sir," Neb pensively replied.

Neb returned to his desk and sat down muttering to himself. He began fidgeting with things on his desk and kept this up for about ten minutes. Finally he turned to me and said, "Bart I want you to do an audit for me." When he called me Bart, I knew that he wanted something. I told him, "Bid told you that he wanted you to do the audit personally." He replied, "I am delegating authority to you to do the audit." I answered , "Nope, Bid told you to do it, I have enough of my own projects to do." Neb turned back to his desk mumbling to himself. He sat their fidgeting for another twenty minutes. He turned back to me and pleaded "Bart, *please do the audit for me.*" I replied," I will do the audit for you on one condition." " What is that? " I told him , "I will do the audit for you if you get off my ass!" Neb promised that he would and I departed for Production line A12.

I talked to the Production Chief for A12. His name is Charles Waters who has been working at the facility for twenty-six years. He was a heavyset man and walked with a limp, he had bushy eyebrows and a wide nose., he talked with a nasal twang ,but his intelligent eyes told me that he was no fool.  He led me to his Expediter, the person who orders parts for the production line, and told him to "Help me in anyway that he can."  I thanked the Production Chief and began to inventory the equipment used on the production line.   In order to perform the audit, one of the many things that I had to do, was to observe the operation of every piece of equipment to insure that they were being utilized according to their operating instructions.   This part of the audit was easier said than done.  Some of the equipment was not in use at that time, so there was a delay while something was found that could be used on the machines.   The Expediter's name was John Barton. John was about forty years old with  gray hair, sharp eyes and his face was slightly wrinkled, indicating that he had aged slightly beyond his years.  I asked John "How long he had been an expediter? "  "Twelve years ", he replied. I then asked him if he had operation and maintenance manuals for all of the equipment  used on the production line?"   He told me " I don't know, you will have to check with Romero Barrera, the Assistant Production Chief."  I talked to Mister Barrera , who was short, chubby but had a twinkle in his eyes, "About the Manuals," he told me, very pensively,  " Some of the equipment is pretty old and the manuals are no longer available for these items."

I gathered up the operation and maintenance manuals that were available and proceeded  with the audit.  I came to an area where a mechanic was performing a maintenance procedure.  The mechanic's name was Eddie Gonzales.  Eddie was about thirty years old with a thin body and face accented by long black hair.  I asked Eddie to demonstrate how he performed his work procedure with the equipment that he was using. Eddie then proceeded to perform his repair function using the equipment. I observed that," There is more that one way that the repair could be accomplished with this equipment, how do you know that you are doing it correctly , when you do not have any specified instructions?" Eddie told me," Charley showed me how to do it". I inquired," Where is Charley now?" "Charley retired four years ago", was Eddie's answer.

It took over a week for me to finish the audit. During that time the only thing that I received from Neb was smiles. I had the secretary type the audit report and then I gave it to Neb. He went rushing off to Bid and proudly presented the audit to him. At he next office meeting, Neb was given a commendation and a three hundred dollar "On The Spot" monetary reward for his excellent work on the audit of Production Line A12.

# CHAPTER 3

A few months later, due to many delays in production, an Inspection Team was sent to the Repair Facility from Washington D.C.. The Inspection Team's three areas of interest were: Management, Productions Lines and Equipment, of course, the area that would impact me directly was Equipment.

The Inspection Team met with all Project Managers. The head of the Inspection Team began by saying, " We are here to help you." The CEO then responded, "We are glad to have you here." The leader of the Inspection Team then outlined their plan for finding causes of the delays in production. They began by scrupulously checking production records, checking maintenance reports, conducting interviews with concerned personnel, but mostly by reading audits that had been done previously by personnel at the Repair Facility.

I was summoned to the Projects Managers office. When I arrived, Bid Brashear and Zeke Humbolt were welcoming a new employee to the office. While I waited to enter the office, I could hear the conversation inside. The new employee was named James Putnam.  James was about six feet tall, with a bushy beard that gave him an appearance of not having a mouth , he had brown eyes with a canopy of bushy eyebrows, making it hard to tell where he was looking. James was saying, " My last position was as Attenuating Analyst for the Development and Enhancement of Upper Management, I am a master of dogmatic solutions and a student of Josie Wales." When James departed the office, both Zeke and Bid agreed that "The boy is brilliant and will go places in the Civil Service Community."

Zeke told me to" Come in and have a seat." I have a list of equipment discrepancies that were found by the Inspection Team from Washington D.C.. He then told me" I want you to go to the Production Lines and document what corrective measures the supervisors are taking to correct the discrepancies." I asked him, "Isn't that the responsibility of another Department?" He told me that "The discrepancies are on equipment, we will handle all matters that concern equipment." I told him "Yes Sir" and departed his office, knowing full well that, if the Production Line Supervisors didn't want to talk to me, there wasn't a darn thing that I could about it.

I shook my head and went off to the Production Lines to get corrective action on the discrepancies, many of which I had found myself, that were listed by the Inspection Team.  Fortunately, I have a pretty good rapport with Production Line Personnel.  Most of the supervisors were cooperative and I didn't have much trouble communicating what I needed from them.  They all told me that," They would send their corrective action measures to Sharon Stonewall", who was coordinating the other actions taken by Production Line Department. Sharon was a very pretty girl whom Mother Nature had generously endowed in appearance, but had slighted her in intelligence. When the time came for me to collect the Corrective Action Reports, I went to see her. When I inquired about the reports, she told me, "I didn't think they were of any importance, so I threw them away." Shaking my head again, I went back to the Production Lines. I managed to retrieve all of the reports from the supervisors, some cheerfully, some begrudgingly.

I told Bid Brasher that "I have all the information required by the Inspection Team."

He told me to, "Make a presentation to take to Washington D.C." I had the secretary type my report, I made projector slides for the key points, and made fifty trifold brochures that described the main end products and listed the important achievements that have been accomplished at the Repair facility.

When I had finished the presentation, I took it to Bid. I asked him "Am I going to give the presentation?" No , Mister Humbolt and I are gong to Washington, D.C. to give the presentation."

Armed with my report and presentation, they were off to the meeting in the Capitol City. Somewhere between the Repair Facility, two airports, two night clubs and their hotel, they lost the presentation. They apologized to the persons that were conducting the meeting for the inefficiency of their staff for not including the required report in their papers, but insured them that the report would be sent to them immediately on their return to the Repair Facility. They did enjoy their visit to the Smithsonian Institute and other points of interest around the city. When they returned, I was summoned to Bid's Office. He said, "Come in, I have something I need to talk to you about." He told me " I need a copy of your Corrective Action Report right away." I inquired, "What happened to the report that you took with you to Washington D.C.?" He informed me that, "The incompetent personnel in Washington D.C. misplaced the report and presentation before he and Zeke could give it." I knew who the incompetent persons were, but I did not give my assesment. I wondered what would happen next.

# CHAPTER 4

It was a hot, muggy August Tuesday, but dark stratus clouds were beginning to form,  ominous weather was looming on the horizon, a hurricane was threating the entire Atlantic Coast.   By all weather predictions, the hurricane would enter our geographic area the following day.   Bid Breashear called an Office meeting to discus the impending  storm with everyone in our office.   He informed us,"Anyone who is not planning on coming to work tomorrow should put in a request for annual leave." Some gullible employees, including myself, did just that. The next day the Repair Facility was closed and the only ones who came in were key Maintenance Personnel.

When the Repair Facility was reopened, everyone was given the word to return to work.  Everyone who did not put in a request for annual leave was given administrative leave, they were given the time off without being charged annual leave.   The employees who did  put in for leave as requested  were charged with annual leave.   Since the employees who did not put in a request for annual leave and did not come into work were granted administrative leave, Leon Cambell took the position, rightfully, that he should be given the administrative leave. Leon went to Bid's office and told him what his feelings were. Bid told him," You can't have the administrative leave because you told me that you were not coming in to work." Leon replied, " No one came in to work" Bid said, "The others intended to come into work." Leon countered, " I intended to come in to work also." "You put in a request for annual leave," Bid replied. " I still want administrative leave!," shouted Leon. "You can't have it!" Bid yelled back. "I want it!",

" You can't have it!" Then Leon shouted " I don't want it!" Bid yelled back, "you're going to get it!" Leon shouted again, " I don't want it! Bid countered with, " You"re going to get it!" Leon then stomped out of Bid's Office and went home. Bid turned to his secretary and said, " I guess I told him."

A Work Student was placed in the office to assist Bid's Secretary. Her name was Galois Roethke. She was about thirty years old and weighed about one hundred and fifty pounds. She had a rounded face and bleached blond hair. She wasn't what you would call attractive but she had a pleasant personality. She did good work if she was told calmly and explicitly what she was expected to do. When she was rushed or spoken harshly to, she became highly agitated and ineffective. Bid did not like her from the day she came into the office. He thought that management was dumping on him by placing her in his office for the summer.

One morning Bid was talking to Neptune Boozer, an

African American who was well schooled in the politics of civil service, everyone called him Nep. Nep worked in the office adjacent to Bid's. Bid said ," Look at that." Nep replied, "Look at what?" Bid gestured toward Galois and said, "Her." " What about her?", asked Nep." " She is ugly! "replied Bid. "Move her into your office, I don't want to have to look at her!" Nep moved her into a desk next to his in accordance with Bid's wishes. Later, Nep confided in me, " Since Bid can't stand ugly, I wonder how he shaves in the morning?"

Two high ranking officers were visiting the Repair Facility to observe operations and get answers to questions on specific items that they were concerned about. They visited all departments including Equipment. The officers met with Zeke Humbolt in the Equipment Projects Office. Since Neptune Boozer and myself were involved with some of the items the officers were inquiring about, we were summoned to Zeke's Office. We knocked and enter the office. Zeke introduced us to the two visitors and then we began our discussion. There were four comfortable chairs arranged in an arc in front of Zeke's Desk. There is also a long couch along one wall. We managed to make eye contact with everyone in the meeting.

We were having a cordial and informative discussion when Bid rushed through the door. He shouted, " Nep, why didn't you tell me that Galois farts?" *"I don't know"*, replied Nep. Then Bid asked,"When did she start doing it and what is her frequency?' *" I don't know!"*, *Nep* repeated. Bid then ran to the couch and said, " I understand that she farts like this.", then he jumped straight up from the couch and shouted, "Phapppppppt." Then he said down

15

and repeated the jump and " Phappppppppt ". Bid then departed the Projects Manager's Office, leaving Zeke trying to look as small as possible and the mouths of our visitors gaping open. I think that we really made an impression on the two officers.

A new man had joined our unit. His name was Lionel Samson. He was transferred to our department awaiting a promotion to a position that would be coming open in the future. He was an amiable person, but he was dumber than dirt, however, management thought that he was the greatest thing since popcorn.

Two weeks later Bid Brashear announced that he was going on extended leave and that Neb Foulcar would be acting in his position while he was on leave. A fellow Employee, Stan Brunner told me, " I heard that Bid is going to have a face lift." I replied," It seems like a waste of money to me." Stan agreed.

Zeke Humbolt called everyone to a meeting in his office. When we had all assembled, he shocked almost everyone in the entire group by announcing that while Neb was acting in Bid Breashear's position, he was going to give Lionel Sampson a paid temporary promotion and move him into Neb's slot until Bid returns. I remained in Zeke's Office after everyone else had departed. I said, I would like to talk to you Mr. Humbolt." Zeke said, " Sure Stinson sit down." I asked him, Why did you put Lionel in Neb's position, there are several capable persons in our unit that could take over for Neb? " Zeke replied, " I feel like Lionel is the best one for the job." I told him, " Besides not being very intelligent, Lionel knows nothing about equipment." Zeke said, " Do You feel that someone in that position should know something about equipment? I replied" Certainly, equipment is what we do, how can you put someone like that in a supervisory position?" Zeke's retort was " He gives me the answers that I want to hear." I replied, " In other words, he knows how to kiss ass." "Yes", Zeke countered. I asked " Is this your criteria for promoting someone, because he knows how to kiss ass?" "That is everyone's criteria here.", was Zeke's answer. I thanked Mr Humbolt for his time and left, more the wiser of policy at this facility.

When Bid returned, Neb came back to his desk and was his usual surley self and the office returned to it's normal humdrum atmosphere. I talked to Stan Brunner about Bid's facelift. Stan said, " He still looks like a Dork." I agreed.

Once again, production delays and cost overruns were in the spotlight at the facility. The CEO hired " Jenkins and Wilkins Consulting Firm" to find out what problems were prevalent at the Repair Facility and recommend solutions and a plan of action for eliminating the difficulties that were presently shedding a bad light on the facility. The cost of hiring the Consulting Firm was over one million dollars.

For six months, A team from the consulting firm meticulously studied Production Records, Production procedures, Personnel Records, and conducted numerous interviews. When the investigation was completed, the Consulting Firm presented their findings to Upper Management of the facility. The report stated," That the skills of the workers was adequate, but the production procedures were inefficiently administered. Their report concluded that the cause of the production delays and cost overruns lies within the management of the organization.

There findings revealed that numerous promotions by nepotism and cronyism has resulted in a facility teeming with supervisors who have inadequate management skills. Many of the supervisors know nothing about the jobs they are supposed to be overseeing  and some can't even read an Instruction Manual.  Management discounted their findings as erroneous and decided to hire another Consulting Firm at a later date, a much later date.

# CHAPTER 5

It was a typical Monday morning, everyone was unenthusiastically going about their redundant every day tasks of the day. Stan Brunner, who is an intelligent young man, in his mid twenties, with sandy hair and a beard to match and I were working on a project together, which was really no more than straightening out routine procurement files. The files had been neglected for a few years and were in a mess. Wendy Ryan came along and asked, "Do you need any help with the files?" I told her, "Thanks, but we have a new and improved filing system that we are implementing." She asked, "Are you sure?" I replied, "Yes, but thank you for asking." When Wendy had left, Stan asked, "What is our new and improved filing system?" I replied, "We will figure that out after we throw out all the old files."

Stan asked me, "Have you thought about your retirement?" I told him, "Not much, it seems like a waste of thought as long as I am working here." Stan replied,

"Yes, I know what you mean, but I don't know where I would go from here." I said, " With my situation here, I would go almost anywhere." Stan lamented." I may have to retire from here." I said with sympathy, "Heaven help you if you have to stay here that long."

We finally cleaned out all the file drawers and had decided which files to keep, when Bid Brashear showed up. He said, "Stop what you are doing and go down to the Production Lines." When you get to the Production lines, ask them"Do you need anything?" I asked Bid, "Can you be a little more specific, they have Procurement Specialists who order their equipment, so what do you have in mind?" Bid roared, "I have already told you too much, now just go do it!" After we had departed the office and were in route to the Production Lines, Stan exclaimed,"There is no doubt in my mind that Scott Adams, the man who created the comic strip "Dilbert", had to work at this facility at one time or another." I agreed.

I started my unusual assignment by talking with Production Line Supervisors. When I asked them, "Do you need any help", most of them looked at me with suspicion and most likely thought that I had been smoking funny weed. They didn't really consider someone from our office as being part of their team. They were polite, but dismissed me with negative answers. I thought to myself, "This is another really meaningful assignment."

I was about to depart the production lines when an electric tractor pulling some small trailers arrived. The driver's name was Mario Russo. Mario's job was to to deliver parts and other items to the Production Lines and pick up items at the Production Lines to deliver to other locations in the facility. Mario was small in stature, had gray hair and a slight accent from the Old Country. He had been working here so long that everyone knew him. I said, "Hello" to Mario and he returned the salutation. "Mario said,"Come here Bart I want to show you something." He produced a picture of a new born baby girl and said,"This is Maria, my ninth grandchild. I gave him the expected response, "She's adorable" and then I asked him, "How old are you Mario?" He answered, "I will be seventy-two next week." I congratulated him and asked, "How long have you worked for the government?" He replied, "Forty-nine years." I asked him, "Why aren't you retired?" He said,"I don't want to retire, some of my kids still live with me and they try to tell me what to do all the time, I would rather be here." I wished him "Happy Birthday" and returned to my office where I would create something meaningful to give Bid.

A few days later, I made a visit to Gabby Geneworth's Office. Gabby is a supervisor in the department where Mario Russo worked. After an exchange of pleasantries and a brief talk concerning my mundane business with him, Gabby told me that, "Mario Russo was finally going to retire." I told Gabby, "I am a little surprised, when did he decide to retire?" Gabby told me,"Mario's sons and daughters called the CEO raising hell because he would not let their father retire." The CEO didn't have a clue as to what brought this on and asked them" What are you talking about?" They replied that Mario told them, "His job was too important for anyone else to do and that the facility would not let him retire." The CEO called Gabby and told him, "Have Mario Russo's retirement papers submitted that afternoon!" Gabby told me,

"Mario's Retirement Ceremony was tomorrow afternoon and that a General from Headquarters was coming to present Mario a citation for his years of service."

The next afternoon everyone that was concerned with Mario's Retirement Ceremony was gathered in the facilities largest Conference Room. Mario, his sons and daughters and grandchildren were seated up front close to the podium. Gabby addressed the audience and proclaimed all of Mario's virtues and contributions to the service of the United States and presented him a plaque and a monetary award. Gabby then introduced General Haygood from headquarters to the audience. The General gave a brief speech and then presented Mario with a citation for his years of service. Mario took the citation, thanked the General, shook his hand and returned to his seat. Mario sat there for a few seconds and then holding his chest he slumped in his chair and fell to the floor. His oldest son yelled,"Dial 911" and began trying to help his father. Medics were called to the Conference Room where they worked with Mario until the EMS Ambulance arrived. The EMS Crew did what they could, administered oxygen and an I V and loaded him into the ambulance. Unfortunately, Mario was pronounced dead on arrival at the hospital. The cause of death was a massive heart attack. Maybe Mario was right, he was better off to keep working.

# Chapter 6

It was a Thursday morning, but it seemed more like a Monday morning. The weather was particularly nasty on this day . Throughout the previous night, fog and rain had prevailed throughout the city and was now continuing on into the day. Visibility was less than one quarter of a mile, slick roads and accidents had made the main travel arteries a virtual parking lot. The tops of the distant mountains could no longer be seen and road signs were almost impossible to read. Many employees were late getting to work due to the hazardous conditions. An inspection team, led by a high ranking official from headquarters was to arrive on this day. Their mission was to inspect two sections that they had determined to be problem areas. Everyone present was speculating on the chances of the group getting to our facility on this day.

One of the employees in our office was named Giuseppe Monteverdi, his friends called him Gus. He was short, portly, very intelligent, had a quick wit and was well liked by everyone, with the exception of a couple of no-minds that were supposed to be supervisors. Intelligence frightened many supervisors at this facility. He went about his work in a professioal manner and didn't bother anyone. He had a lot of experience working with the government and only asked to be left alone while he was doing his job. He was summoned to Bid Brashear's office on this morning, after a lengthy meeting with Mr. Brashear, he returned to his desk. He walked over to my desk and asked, "Are you busy?" I told him. "I am no more busy than usual, what is on your mind?" He said that, "They are having some sort of problems with some equipment on Production Line A12 and I have been assigned to find and correct whatever they are." He said, "You have had a lot of experience with Production Line A12, would you like to come along with me?" I told him, "Sure, I want to get out of the office for awhile anyway."

We walked, ever alert to the parts trains and fork lifts that roamed the halls. The drivers drove with their eyes transfixed straight ahead, oblivious to anything on either side of them. A person did not want to make the mistake of stepping in front of them. There was an incident where Neptune Boozer was standing on a corner, when a tractor driver pulling three wagons ran over his foot and continued on his merry way, never suspecting that he had injured someone.

As we walked, Gus told me of a project that he was doing. Gus was always inventing or improving convenience devices. He told me that, "He needed a strap wrench, but he couldn't find one." I told him "I do not have one but there is a tool room in Production Line

A12 Area and maybe he could borrow one there."

We arrived at Production Line A12 and went to the tool room first.   Charles Higgenbottom was the Tool room Manager.   Charles was about forty years old with graying blond hair and a bushy mustache.   Gus said "Hi Charles, I am looking for an old tool that I haven't seen in years."   Charles replied, "If you lose some of that belly, you will be able to see it."   Gus replied "Smart ass!, seriously, I need a strap wrench do you have one?"   Charles told him that " I do not have one and do not know of anyone who would have one in the facililty."   Gus said ,"Thanks anyway" and then we went to see Romero Barrera.   We arrived at his office and was asked to come in.   We exchanged greetings with the usual cordialness and then Gus asked him "Which  pieces of equipment are you having trouble with?"   Mr Barrera told us "We are having problems mainly with the shaper."   He then led us down onto the Production Line to the shaper.   Romero introduced us to Wendell Collier, the operator of the shaper and a new employee.

Gus asked Wendell, 'What is the problem that you are having?"   He told us," When the parts are measured by the NC Machine, they are out of tolerance.   I told him, I have performed an audit on the shaper and it was working very good at that time."   I Asked him. "Where is your operating manual?"   Wendell looked puzzled and then starting opening doors on the machine and searching for the manual.   He came up with the instruction book and asked. "Is this it?"   Gus said, "You don't know this is the operating manual?"   Wendell said," I never use it."   I said,"Go ahead and show us how you perform this procedure."   As Wendell was operating the shaper, Gus and I were reading the operating manual. When he was finshed, I asked him,"Why did you do it that way?"

"That is the way I was told to do it" he replied. "That is not the way the operating manual instructs to do it, Gus said. I said to him," Just read the operating manual, page number nine", as I showed the page to him. A look of panic came on to his face , "I am going to tell my supervisor!, "Wendell cried. He ran to Mr. Barrera's Office and returned with him. Romero asked. "What is the problem here?" We explained that Wendell was not following the procedures in the operating manual and asked him to walk through the procedure with him. Mr. Barrera took the manual and instructed Wendell how to do the procedure. When the procedure was over we took the piece to the NC Room and measured it, the part met all specifications. We told Mr. Barrera that Wendell needed more instructions on operating the machine. Romero, somewhat embarrassed, said, "He will have more training right away." When we left the area, Gus said," I don't think that training will do Wendell much good." I replied, "I don't either, it is obvious that Wendell can not read."

To our surprise, when we arrived back at our office, the Inspection Team from Headquarters was present there. Gus said , "I did not think that they were supposed to inspect our office." I replied, "They were not." Zeke Humbolt was there talking to members of the Inspection Team. When we approached them , Zeke introduced us to the head of the team, Brigadier General Napoleon Lysander, a man of about sixty years, about five feet nine inches tall, a little over weight, with gray hair and a mustache to match. He looked a little disheveled,  his hat and the rest of his uniform were showing the effects of having been out in the rain.   When he spoke to us, his manner and tone of voice implied that his opinion was correct and no one had better question his authority. He told us, "We dropped-in on your office to dry off, we have gotten soaked walking around in this weather.  He said, "My socks are particularly wet from wading around in the streets here, I am going to dry them out in the microwave oven."  Stan Brunner stated, "I don't think that that is a really good idea." The General replied, "Of course it is, the microwave will quit heating when the moisture is removed from the socks." He then proceeded to remove his socks and put them into the microwave oven.  He set the timer on the microwave for ten minutes and then went off to talk to Zeke Humbolt.  Someone saw smoke billowing out of the microwave and yelled, "

Theres a fire!"  Someone yelled , "Call the Fire Department!"   One of the secretarys called the Fire Department and then shouted, "I am getting out of here!"  Almost everyone started running for one of the doors.  The general heard the commotion and ran to the microwave where his socks were on fire and blazing nicely. He grabbed a trash can which was full of paper and opened the microwave door.  He grabbed the microwave heating plate and dumped the burning socks into the trash can, where the paper inside ignited and blazed almost to the ceiling.  Someone shouted , "The place is going to burn down!" The General run around in a little circle, trying to figure out what to do.  Stan Brunner then calmly picked-up the coffee pot and emptied it into the trash can  extinguishing the fire.  About the time the fire was extinguished, a fire axe came crashing through the main entrance door, followed by firemen rushing into the room with a fully charged fire hose. They were hosing down everything and everbody looking for the fire.

Finally they shut-off the fire hose nozzle and asked, "Where is the fire?" Stan pointed at the trash can and said, "The fire is out now." The firemen gathered around the trash can and stared at it briefly, after determining the fire was no longer a threat, they left the office carrying their fire hose. They removed what was left of the main entrance door and set it aside. The general, who was now thoroughly soaked, with water streaming down on his face from his hat , his bare feet inserted into his wet shoes, took his entourage and departed for Headquarters.

# CHAPTER 7

There was a fellow employee in the office named Clifford Backstreet, he was short and pudgy, with beady eyes and a very short hair cut, no one paid much attention to him, but he had a plan. He was going get promoted by assmosis, "the process of getting ahead by continually sucking up to management." He did indeed become the champion Brown Noser in the office. He did not contribute much to accomplishment of the work load shared by fellow employees, because he spent much of the work day following around and licking the boots of anyone that he thought could help him accomplish his goal. Some of the persons carrying his load complained, but management did not say much to him, as he was inflating their egos daily. Then one day all his groveling and kissing-up paid off. A promotion opened up in the office and he got it. He became supervisor of one of the teams in the office and he became a little "Caesar". He told himself, " Now I will show them". He talked to the personnel under his supervision as if they were Army recruits.

One morning he was being particularly caustic with a fellow named Ben White. Ben decided enough was enough, he jumped up and shouted, " You talk to me like that again you fat little jerk and I will screw your head into the floor!" Clifford ran as fast as he could to Bid Brashears Office, "Shouting that he had been threatened!" Bid summoned Ben to his office for counseling. As the weeks passed, Ben and others were summoned to Bid's office for the same reason. Ben confided in me that, "Before backstreet had become supervisor, he had hardly talked to Bid Breashear, but now he is beginning to feel like they are real buddies" He said that " I spend so much time in Bid's Office that I might as well move my desk in there."

Bid knew that he had to do something about Backstreet, but he had promoted him and didn't want to do anything that would bring embarrassment to himself. He was in a quandary trying to figure out what to do, when a solution presented itself. The installation was under going another reorganization, this time the motto was SIGMA TEN. In time SIGMA would come to symbolize the acronym "Silly, Ignorant, Gullable Management Assholes" to the workers who had to live with the changes made under this reorganization. The reorganization was triggered by the abrupt removal of the Installations CEA, who was found culpable of something, information was scarce as to the reason he was removed. The word was that he was either going to be fired, put into jail or banished to an installation in Alaska, I never found out what his real fate was. A representative from each department would form a team to insure that the changes of the reorganization would be implemented in a smooth and orderly fashion. This presented Bid Brashear with the opportunity to get rid of Clifford Backstreet without Putting an inference to his flawed judgement. Of course, he assigned Clifford to the reorganization team. Fortunately, during the time that Clifford was assigned to the team, he obtained a position with another Government Agency and never returned to the office.

Winter was swiftly approaching, there are times when the temperature can be bitterly cold in this area. The snow plows and rock salt trucks sometimes have a hard time keeping the streets clear when blizzards blow in from the north. On this day, there was a nice blanket of snow on the ground, but the temperature was warming up and the snow was melting. I was wondering how the reorganization was going to affect me, when Stan Brunner came up to me and asked, "Have you heard the latest?" I told him that, " I am always the last to know about anything that goes on around here." "We are going to have to move", he told me. "*Terrific,*" I replied, "Where are they going to exile us to this time?" Stan told me that, "We are going to be moved to the old Engineering Offices at the back of the complex. I said, "That is really great, the place is drafty as a barn and the heat doesn't work half of the time!" I asked him, "Whose brainstorm brought all of this about?" Stan said' "It was the Interim CEA's idea, he wants to move all of the offices concerned with the Production Lines into one area, making it one big super Production line Office. The Small Parts Office below us is going to have to move also, because their offices will be encompassed into the Production Line Office." Stan told me, Hammond Burger has been appointed Director of the Production Line office." Hammond was a real "mover and shaker", he liked to micromanage everything. I had heard complaints from some of the employees that worked for him about him wanting to see every piece of paper that they dealt with and the topic of all telephone conversations that they made. Hammond was afraid that with his new office being on the top floor and part of the office being on the ground floor, that he couldn't get down the stairs quick enough to keep his finger on the pulse of everything that was going on. Then he got an idea that would solve this perplexity. He would have a fireman's pole installed from the top floor to the ground floor, then he could respond quickly to any situation that occurs on the ground floor.

That night, with the clear skies, the temperature plummeted to five degrees above zero. Now there was a nice sheet of ice on everything. The next morning Bid Brashear called an office meeting. He told everyone that we had to move today because the Production Line Office Personnel wanted to to start moving their office equipment into the space that they were going to occupy. Someone asked Bid " When are the Riggers going to be here?" He replied that "They are not coming today, they said that it is too dangerous for them to move around outside." Someone asked Bid, "Then how are the Production Line people going to move into here?" Bid said caustically, "That is their problem!" Stan asked Bid."How are we going to move our office equipment if the Riggers aren't coming?" Bid said."Put your desk items in boxes, I have my orders and we can get the rest of our stuff later." Luckily, Steve Warren, a fellow employee, had a van and was willing to transport our boxes and computer equipment to our new location. It was a very perilous task to get the boxes and other items from one building to another while trying to keep our balance on the slick surface. The computers, printers, faxes etc. were stacked in a corner where they would remain for four days. The installations  computer whiz was Larry Ferule. It took him four days to straighted out the computer cables and get connected to the LAN, making our computer system operational. The telephone people also took four days to get our telephones installed. Meanwhile, Boxes were serving as desks and buckets and other boxes were serving as desk chairs.  In the interim, a lot of hand scribing, almost a lost art, was performed.  Anytime someone had to make a phone call, a trip through the slush to another building to borrow a telephone was made.  Finally our desks, chairs and tables arrived and were set up in a workable configuration  and everything returned to almost normal, which was total chaos.

Three months later Hammond Burger had his office set up to his specifications, including the fireman's pole, and was ready for any emergency.  Finally, the chance to use his rapid transit system came, a supervisor in the office on the ground floor, Tim Butcus, called and told Hammond, " That they had a situation that called for Mr. Burgers attendance." Hammond hung up the phone and ran to the fireman's pole and leaped on it, , where he shot like a bullet to the ground floor.  He was laying on the floor in agony, as the office personnel on the ground floor gathered around him to see what happened. Then they saw it, there was an oil stain down the front of Hammond's clothes and oil on his hands. Someone had made sure that Mr. Burger would get to the ground floor very quickly. He was laying on the floor in pain for thirty minutes before the paramedics arrived and took him away. The next day the fireman's pole was removed and the hole in the top floor was blocked off until repairs could be made.

# CHAPTER 8

It was a gorgeous morning. The brutal winter had finally moved on for another year. The sun was shining and all the world seemed in harmony. I was in one of my favorite places, a secluded part of the woods where a small stream meandered happily over rocks that gave it an effervesce that created a very relaxing atmosphere. Some Tufted Titmice in a nearby oak tree were fussing at a Blue Jay that had just alighted near them. Dragon Flies were were practicing touch and go landings on the stream, pausing momentarily on the water's surface and then lifting -off and circling until their next contact with the water. Oak leaves that looked like tiny sail boats were bobbing down the stream on their voyage to the big river. This was a place that I could truly relax and forget the troubles and anxieties of the everyday rat race.

That morning my alarm clock had startled me awake at the usual workday time. In a state of somnolence, I pushed the snooze button and put my pillow over the clock. When the somewhat less irritating sound of the alarm sounded once again, I told myself, "I can not go to work today." After three cups of coffee to get my eyes open, I took a shower and then called my boss. I told him that, "I have some urgent business to attend to today and I will not be able to come into work, put me on leave and I will see you tomorrow." I did have an urgency, I needed some time off from the back-stabbing politics and inane activities that awaited me at my employment location. I knew that I would have to face it all tomorrow, but today was my day to clear my mind and recharge my energy for whatever awaited me. Through the years, my job had been pretty low profile. My assignments did not include any travel and except for rare occasions, meetings with anyone that wasn't an employee of the repair facility was never in my itinerary, most of my activities were the routine tasks that kept the wheels turning at the repair facility, but like many others, I did not receive recognition for my work and did not become anyone's hero.

While I was relaxing, there was something happening in the office that would have an impact on my welfare. Zeke Humbolt had just returned from a meeting with the CEA.

With a scowl on his face, he called Bid Brashear to his office. When Bid arrived, Zeke told him, "I have just been assigned the impossible, the facility sold a MoronUT18 to the Navy in India., now the thing isn't working and the whole problem has been dumped on me, I don't know if there is anyone here who can fix it or not. " Bid said, "Don't look at me, I haven't a clue as to what the thing is supposed to do!" "If I send someone over there and they botch the job, it will really look bad for me, this could be a diplomatic disaster! ," shouted Zeke. Bid said, "We need to send someone that can be a scapegoat if the Indian Navy isn't satisfied." Who do you recommend?" Bid said, "Stinson seems to know as much about repair equipment as anyone and he is expendable, if he can't fix the thing." "Yes, I believe that Stinson is the right person to send over there, I will tell the CEA that I am sending my top man", Zeke said with a Grinch-like smile.

The next day Zeke Humbolt's secretary called and said that Zeke Humbolt wanted to see me. I walked to his office, knocked on his door and entered. "Good morning Mr. Humbolt" I said, as cordially as I could. He Replied, "Sit down Stinson, there is something I want to talk to you about." Zeke asked me, "How much traveling have you done since ylou have been here?" I replied, "Very little, just some trips to training sites." He said "You are one of the very few of my employees who are not married. How would you like an assignment that will take you about a month over seas?" The month away from the facility sounded good, but I feared that ther was a catch. I told Mr. Humbolt that , "I will go to any location that my assignments take me." "Good, I need a specialist with your expertise to go to India." I asked, "What is happening in India?" Zeke replied, "The government sold a MoronUT18 to the Indian Navy to repair aircraft aboard their aircraft carrier, the equipment is not working and the Indian Navy is pretty upset." I asked, "Why doesn't the company who built it send a Factory Representative over their to solve the problem or just give them a new one?" Zeke said "United Algamated has bought the company and has discontinued the

MoronUT18." "Why does the responsibility for the equipment fall on us?" I asked. Zeke replied, " The equipment came from this facililty." "When do I go over there?" I asked. Zeke said, "Right away, see Jenkins in the Administration Office and he will make all the travel and financial arrangements for you." I thanked Mr. Humbolt for the assignment and departed for the Administration Office. It seemed like A good opportunity but, I had a bad feeling in my stomach.

I went to the Administration office and asked for Mr. Jenkins. A coworker in the office directed me to his location, which was located to the rear. I found him sitting at a desk in the back of the office. When he saw me he motioned for me to come to his desk. When I arrived, he greeted me, "Hello Bart, I have been expecting you, I have been working on your itinerary." Jenkins was about five feet six inches tall, with a pale complexion, portly and his grayish hair was balding on the back of his head, his bottom had spread, attesting to the many years sitting at a desk. "You are going on quite a trip, I wish that I could get one like that." I replied, "You had better wait and see how this trip goes before you wish for something like that." He said, "I have your transportation mapped out, I am waiting for your airline tickets to arrive now. You will fly to Dallas on United Airlines, where you will catch a flight on American Airlines to Sacramento and then fly Pan American Airlines to Delhi, India. From there you will ride trains to Bombay, "where the carrier " INS Gandhi" is stationed." He further explained, "In Delhi, you can catch a train on the Northern Railroad to Kanpur, where you will catch a train on the Central Railway to Indore. There you will catch a train on the

Western Railway to Bombay. I said. "Wait a minute, you mean that there is no airline flights to Bombay!" Bombay is now called "Mumbai". He said, "I was told to make the travel arrangements as inexpensive as possible." I informed him that, "I am not the sharpest pencil in the box, but that I was not going to travel all the way across India on trains, either I get a flight to Bombay or I am not going." "I will tell that to anyone, including the CEO." Jenkins told me "I will see what I can do." I left and went back to my office. Shortly after I arrived there I received a call from Jenkins telling me that he had a flight for me. I went back to his office, knocked and went in. Jenkins said, "Bart, I have a flight to Bombay (Mumbai) on Air India. " I have arranged for a rental car with Avis through OPODO, when you arrive in Mumbai. You can see Sheila for a voucher for your travel money." I thought to myself, My travel itinerary was pretty complicated, but the government works in mysterious ways, it is still pretty complicated, but not as bad as it was. I did not know that Zeke Humbolt had told Jenkins to make my trip as miserable as possible. I thanked Mr. Jenkins for his efforts and then went to see Sheila. I picked-up my voucher and then went to the Disbursing Office and got my money.

The day came for my departure to India. I had, in the meantime, obtained my passport and VISA and received the required shots. I wasn't sure of what would be the proper attire for India, but I was pretty sure that it would be hot. I packed what light clothes that I had and hoped that they would suffice for whatever I had to do when I arrived there. I checked my luggage curbside and went through the routine metal detector and then proceeded on to the departure gate to the Dallas Fort Worth (DFW)

Airport.. My flight to DFW was comfortable enough, except for my cramped legs, but everything was routine and the airplane arrived on time at the DFW Airport. I had checked my luggage through to Sacramento, so all that I had to do was amuse myself for the next four hours while I waited for my next flight. I have never found a way to get comfortable in an airport. I bought a magazine and tried to be interested in it until time for my flight.

Finally, it was time for my departure from DFW to Sacramento. It was a four hour flight to get there. The Flight Attendants were courteous and provided me with one of the little pillows that they had an abundance of. After the plane was in the air, we were given the beverage of our choice and a "mystery meat" sandwich. I wasn't sure what it was, so I didn't eat it. I looked at the "American Way" magazine which was deposited in the pocket on the back of the seat in front of me. I did the puzzle in the magazine and then nodded off for a little nap. I was awakened by announcements on the loud speaker to "Buckle your seat belts and Flight Attendants prepare for landing." There was also a list of departure gates for connecting flights. The landing was smooth and it wasn't long before we arrived at the departure gate. I retrieved my luggage from the Baggage Claim Area and then discovered that I had to go through security again to get back into the main terminal. At the terminal entry gate, I was wanded with a metal detector, patted down and was required to show two forms of identifications. I thought for a minute I was going to be strip searched. An hour later, when the security personnel were finally satisfied, I was free to continue on into the terminal.

I checked my luggage in the main terminal and then went on to the departure gate for India. When I arrived at the departure gate, I was informed by an attendant "That I was late and the flight had already departed." I was also told that "There would not be another until 2:00 PM the next day. " Since there was no alternative, I resigned myself to the fact that I would have to spend the night there, but not at the Airport. I have had to spend a miserable night at an Airport and I wasn't about to do it again. I caught a taxi to a nearby hotel, where I spent the night. Luckily, I carried some extra socks and underwear in the brief case that I always have with me. The next day I had breakfast at the hotel and was back at the airport by nine o'clock. I wasn't going to take any chances on being held up by security again. This time I was waved through a metal detector and I was on my way to the departure gate for my flight to India. It was a long, boring morning but, when it came time for the plane to depart, I had no problem with Customs Officials, after I had shown them my passport and VISA, I was waved on through the Departure Gate and boarded the airplane. At last, I was on my way to India.

A tall brunette Flight Attendant offered to hang-up my suit coat for me, I left it in her capable hands and proceeded on back to the back of the plane to find my seat, which was by the window. After all the passengers were aboard, the two seats next to me were empty, the plane was loaded to about three fourths capacity. The plane taxied out on a runway, where we waited for thirty minutes for the pilot to get clearance to take off. During this interval, the Flight Attendants informed the passengers of the emergency exits and how to use the oxygen masks in case of a loss of pressure. The plane proceeded slowly until it made a right turn on the runway, then we took off. The plane began moving slowly and then the engines reached a high pitch and the plane picked-up speed. My back was pressed against the back of my seat as the plane hurtled down the runway and then rose into the air. I looked out the window at the quickly disappearing coastline as the plane rapidly gained altitude. After that, all I could see was the ocean. Having served in the United States Navy, I had seen the ocean before and quickly lost interest in looking out the window. After the airplane had reached cruising altitude, the Flight attendants pushed their drink carts down the aisles, offering everyone the beverage of their choice. I asked for a coke and purchased a little bottle of rum to go in it. Later on, the Flight Attendants came around with trash bags collecting plastic cups and empty cans and little bottles. I then occupied myself by reading a not so interesting novel that I had bought at the airport. Three hours into the flight the Flight Attendants once again pushed their drink carts down the aisles, serving drinks and the in-flight meal. The meal consisted of some kind of chicken and potato salad, I think, and a small lettuce salad. I ate the salad and decided I really wasn't hungry enough to eat the rest of it. Later the Flight Attendants came around again with trash bags and collected the drink containers and meal trays. Although the seats were not very comfortable, I had plenty of room and decide to try to take a nap. I can never really get comfortable with my shoes on, so I kicked them off. A pretty, young blond Flight Attendant came down the aisle. I stopped her and asked for a pillow. She smiled and promptly retrieved a pillow for me. I settled down for my nap and got as comfortable as possible. I was just dozing off, when I felt some kind of warm liquid pouring onto my foot. There was a black lady sitting in the seat in front of me holding a boy of about two years old. Her dress was now well anointed with urine, as was my right foot. I got up and retrieved my brief case from the overhead bin. I removed a pair of socks and returned the briefcase to the overhead bin. I took off my socks and put on the dry ones. I then deposited the wet socks in a "barf bag" and left them for a trash pick-up. I decided that it would be wise to keep my shoes on for the rest of the flight. When the airplane started it's descent for landing, an announcement was made on the loud speaker, "For all passengers to put their seats and trays in the upright position and buckle their seat belts, and for the Flight Attendants to prepare for landing." The pilot made a nice smooth landing and then taxied to Terminal II at the Indira Gandhi International Airport. When it was time for the passengers to deplane, I retrieved my suit coat and wandered out into the terminal building with the rest of the passengers. I followed the other passengers to the Baggage Claim and retrieved my suitcase. I also found a counter where I could change some greenbacks into rupees. The exchange rate was about eighty rupees to a dollar.

The terminal was filled with travelers from many countries. The airport serves 9500 International Flights and 13,100 Domestic Flights every day. I moved out into the crowd in search of Air India for my final flight to Mumbai. I had trouble reading the signs and monitors and began to feel a little lost. I observed a lady, whom

I believed to be English. I approached her and asked, "If she could help me?" She replied in a precise English accent,"I would be happy to." I told her that my next flight was to Mumbai on Air India and I wasn't sure where to go." She told me " Air India departs from Terminal 1A and directed me to how to get there." She was a handsome woman probably in her fifties with silver hair and beautiful blue eyes and a broad smile that made her face light up. She was dressed in smart light tan tweed suit, brown shoes and a tan scarf, a truly impressive woman. I told her"Thank you very much" and proceeded on to Terminal 1A to search for the gate for my flight to Mumbai.

At Teminal 1A, I was able to find the gate where my flight would depart. An Air India Attendant told me that the flight would not leave for four hours. I checked my bag and then left the ticket counter in search of something to eat. I found a resturant called the Sarovar. I went in, found a table and a waitress promptly came to take my order. I ordered something called Bhindi Masala, saag paneer and velvety lamb Vindaloo, which had a mixture of vegetables, okra was one that I recognized, and some kind of meat, supposedly lamb. It wasn't really to my taste, but it was better than Airline food. When I finished the meal I gave the waitress the money for my meal, which was about twenty-five dollars, and went back to the gate to wait for my flight. While I was waiting for my flight to depart, I read some more in my not so interesting novel. The announcement came for the boarding of the airplane to Mumbai. The passengers got in line to show their tickets and moved out onto the tarmac for boarding. We walked to the boarding ladder and up into the aircraft. We were greeted by three flight attendants who looked like triplets. The were all about five feet two inches tall with dark eyes and bright white teeth that made their faces light-up when they smiled. They were dressed in dark blue uniforms with white blouses underneath Nehru type jackets and ankle length skirts. They were very accommodating, but I wasn't quite sure what they were saying. Anyway, I found my seat and settled-in for the flight to Mumbai. It took about an hour from time of boarding to touching down at Mumbai International Airport. It was a pretty smooth flight and I congratulated the pilot after he taxied to the arrival gate and everyone started departing the aircraft. I entered the airport with a feeling of trepidation because I did not know what fate awaited me now that I had reached Mumbai.

# CHAPTER 9

I managed to find the baggage claim and waited for my luggage to arrive. I waited and waited and waited, but my suitcase did not arrive. I saw one of the personnel who brought out the baggage. I approached him to inquire about my luggage. He waved his hands and shook his head, because he did not speak English. I found another worker who could speak English. He told me that "I should go to the Air India ticket counter," and gave me directions on how to get there. When I arrived at the ticket counter, there was a pretty long line, so I took my place in line, I did not want to appear rude to the people in a country that I had never been before. After a lengthy wait, I reached the counter' where a tall man with a narrow face and a broad smile, at least I think he was smiling, asked " Are you American?" I replied "I am" and told him of my problem with my lost luggage. He produced a form with many languages on them, fortunately, English was one of them.. He apologized for the inconvenience and told me "Fill out this paper and bring it back to me." I filled in the appropiate blanks including the hotel where I would be staying, which was the Ramada Plaza Palm Grove. I returned to the end of the counter waved my new friend over and gave him the lost luggage form. I then moved out into the terminal searching for the car rental stations. I passed one of the main entrance doors and went outside the terminal. Mumbai is the largest and busiest city in India. The streets were packed with all kinds of vehicles. I decided to forego the car rental and catch a taxi to my hotel. There was some yellow and black taxis lined-up by the entrance. As I walked up to them, a driver jumped out of his cab and came to meet me. He was about five feet six inches tall with a pug nose and bright white teeth that showed gold inlays when he smiled. "You need taxi?" ,he said. "Yes", I replied. "My name Rajah, where you want to go?" ,he asked. "I want to go to the Ramada Plaza Palm Grove Hotel, I told him. "Yes, it is out by Juhu Beach, I take you there", he said. He eased out into the swarm of vehicles that seemed to be one continuous traffic jam. It confirmed my decision to waive the privlidge of using a rental car to be a good one. The trip from the airport took about forty-five minutes and cost about twelve dollars. I gave the fare and a five hundred Rupee tip to Rajah. "Will you be going out later?" he asked. "Yes I have to buy some clothes", I told him. "I wait for you", He said. "I would appreciate it" I replied.

The hotel looked like a big seven story box with windows, but there were several people going and coming through the main entrance. I entered the lobby and went to the reception counter. An English speaking  clerk, who was tall with sharp eyes and a long chin came to greet me. "May I help you", he asked. I told him who I was and that I had a reservation. He said," Yes mister Stinson, you will be in room three twelve, I have you listed for three nights." " I told him "I hope that will be enough time to complete my work here" He told me, "If you need an extension of your days here, that it would not be a problem" and then he reminded me that it would be $110.00 per night. He asked, "Do you have your luggage?" I told him "My luggage was lost on the flight to Mumbai." I am very regretful to hear that" he sympathized. He gave me the key to my room. I looked the hotel over as I left the desk and proceeded to my room. It had two restaurants and lounges, a pool, spa and steam room. I arrived at my room and went in. It was a nice room with a king size bed, a small refrigerator and a coffee maker. I put my breifcase in a dresser drawer and left the hotel to look for Rajah.

True to his word, I found Rajah parked a short distance from the entrance to the hotel.

I approached his taxi and he jumped out to meet me. "Where you like to go?", he asked. I asked him "Do you know where I can buy some clothes?" He replied, "Yes, I take you there." He merged into the traffic, no small task, as the streets were filled with motorcycles, pedicabs,trucks, taxis, large and small cars. After about forty minutes of maneuvering through the traffic on the crowded streets, we came to the "Mahatma Jyotiba Phule Market". Rajah exclaimed, "This market opened in 1860, you can buy anything here, I wait for you." He hurried around the taxi and opened the door for me. I thanked him and proceeded into the crowded market.

There were numerous fruit and vegetable stands and kiosks displaying all kinds of fabrics among a myriad of sellers of other items. I found a clothing store and went in. I was approached by a short balding man who walked with a limp, but he was dressed in a stylish suit. "You are an American", he said. "Yes I am", I replied, "I need to buy some clothes." The man said "Ah yes, we can make you the finest suit in India." I told him "No thanks, I have a suit, I need something to work in." He sounded disappointed as he said," I am sure that we can find something for you." I finally ended up purchasing a khaki shirt with four pockets and a pair of matching khaki trousers, also with an ample number of pockets. As I looked into a full length mirror, I said to myself, "Just call me Bwana." I purchased two of the "Jungle Jim" outfits and three pairs of socks. I then started back to find Rajah. As I walked through the throng of human bodies in the market, I was amazed at the variety of wares that were available there. I found Rajah and told him to take me back to the hotel. When we arrived at the hotel, I asked Rajah, "Do you know where the INS Gandhi is docked?" He replied, Oh yes, it is at the Vizag Dockyard, I can take you there." I told him, "I want to go there at eight o'clock in the morning, how long will it take to get there? He said, "About two hour." I said "Terrific, better make that six o'clock" "I be here Mr. Stinson." I told him "Just Bart will do." he replied, "Yes Mr. Bart" I paid him the fare plus a five hundred rupee tip and then entered the hotel.. At the hotel's Gift Shop, I bought a tooth brush, tooth paste, some disposable razors and some shaving cream. I also purchased a small zipper bag to put my work clothes in. I had not planned on working my first day on the ship, but after finding out how far away I was, I wanted to try to solve their problem in one day. I certainly did not want to make any more trips than necessary across the country. I managed to get a pizza , at least that is what it was supposed to be, at a snack bar and then returned to my room.

I had a wake-up call for five AM the next morning, but I was already awake, thinking with a feeling of apprehension about what lay ahead of me on my mission in this strange land.

I had a light breakfast at one of the restaurants and then equipped with breif case and zipper-bag I departed the hotel. I found him in approximately the same place that he was parked yesterday, when we went to the market. Rajah jumped out of the cab and said "Hi Mister Bart", at least he didn't call me Sahib. I replied, "Good morning Rajah, we had better get started." Rajah merged with the throng of vehicles and we were on our way out of Mumbai. After we left gthe city proper, we entered a two lane road where the congestion made for slow driving. To join the traffic we encountered in the city, there were now cattle carts , tractor drawn wagons, pedestrians and loose cattle that seemed to have the right of way over anything else. The trip took close to three hours to reach the dockyard. With Rajah's help, I managed to tell a guard what we were there for. Rajah drove us as close as he could to the INS Gandhi. There was another aircraft carrier there, the INS Viraat. The Viraat was purchased from the British, and as Aircraftr Carriers go, it was a pretty old design. There was a large scoop on the bow of the ship to give the aircraft  lift to get into the air when they left the flight deck of the carrier. The INS Viraat displaced about 28,700 tons, which was much smaller than the INS Gandhi. The Gandhi was a newer ship with a Conning Tower and flight deck comparable to United States Aircraft Carriers.

I told Rajah that I did not know how long it would take for me to complete my business on the ship. Rajah said, "I wait for you." I told him, "Keep the meter running" I gave him three thousand rupees and told him, "We will settle the rest when we get back to the hotel." Rajah repeated, "I wait for you." Equipped with my briefcase and small zipper bag, I proceeded on to my adventure aboard an Indian ship. I walked a few feet and turned and waved to Rajah, not knowing that I would never see him again.

# CHAPTER 10

I walked on down to where the Gandhi was docked. The gangway to the ship was two sets of stairs with a platform in the middle and one on the top which was connected to the hangar deck which was the acting quarterdeck where the Officer-Of-The-Deck was stationed. I made my way up to the top of the gangway where the Officer-Of-The-Deck came to meet me. I said, "Request permission come aboard sir?" He looked at me rather strangly, but motioned for me to come on board. He was about five feet eight inches tall with a broad nose and sharp eyes. I was not familiar with uniforms of the Indian Navy, so I wasn't sure what his rank was. I think it was the equivilent of a Lieutenant Junior Grade in the United States Navy. He spoke very little English and I did not speak any Hindi, the national language of India, so it made it difficult to communicate. With the help of the papers I had with me and a young orderly, who was on duty with the Officer-Of-The-Deck, I was able to tell him why I was there. The orderly walked over to a shipboard announcing system and spoke into the microphone. His announcment reverbrated from the speakers throughout the ship. I could not understand most of what he said, but I think it was for Left Tenenant Barase to come to the quarterdeck.

A short time late, an officer walked onto the quarterdeck. He was slightly undersix feet tall, with narrow cheeks and piercing eyes. He looked very professional and sharp in his uniform. His shoes were polished to a high shine and the brass on his uniform was also. He asked, "Are you Mr. Stinson?" When I nodded that I was, he said, " We have been expecting you, my name is Rang Barase, I will be your Liaison Officer while you are here." He spoke with a precise English accent. I asked him, "Where did you go to school, you speak very good English?" He replied "I graduated from Eton College in England." I told him, "I could tell that you have a good education." He told me, "I also have an Engineering Degree from "Thodomal Shahani Engineering College" here in Mumbai." I said , "I am impressed." I asked him," is there someplace that I could change out of my suit into some working clothes before we go to the equipment  that I was there to repair?" At least I hoped that I could repair it. He told me that I could have the use of his stateroom while I was on the ship. He led me to his stateroom, which turned out to be beneath the steam catapult room for launching aircraft. In the stateroom there was a small desk and table,  2 full length lockers, two bunk beds, upper and lower and a small safe. Rang said, "you can use the locker on the left to put your things in while you are on the ship."

After I had changed into my khakis, we departed his stateroom to go back to the hangar deck, where the equipment that they were having trouble with was located. The apparatus was across the ship and forward of the quarterdeck. We arrived at the site where the instrument was connected to electricity, I got my first look at the "mystry machine" that I was supposed to repair. A crewman that was about forty-five years old with slightly graying hair and wrinkles under his eyes, high-lighting his swarthy complexion, had been summoned to the location before we arrived. Rang told me that the man's name was Lok Sabah and that he was in charge of most of the testing performed on the aircraft. I asked, "Does he speak English?" Rang replied, He speaks bloody little English!" I said to Rang, "Tell him that I need the operating and repair manual for the equipment." After a considerably long discussion Rang told me,"The manual was read to him by an interpreter and sense he could not read it, the manual was no longer in his possession and he did not know where it is." I said to Rang, "Tell him to turn it on and lets see what it does." Lok plugged in a connecting cable to an aircraft and turned on the equipment. After a discussion between Rang and Lok, I was informed that the evaluation read-outs did not light up on the status board. There were several other lights on the equipmet that I did not understand, but all of them seemed to be dim. I said " I will look inside the instrument to try to locate the problem" Lok produced a screw driver, with which I could remove the screws that held the inspection plate in place. I removed the inspection plate and examined the inside of the instrument. I said to myself, " Please don't let it be a circuit board." I clearly did not know what I was looking at, but I could not see any obvious damage to the apparatus. Some kind of emphatic announcement came over the loud speakers. Rang said "I have to leave now but I will catch up with you later." He departed the area and so did Lok. There I sat, all alone on a foreign ship wondering what that I should do next. I carry a small multimeter in my brief case for measuring volgtage and resistance on various types of equipment. The test equipment is supposed to operate on 230 volts. I got a reading of only 190 volts coming into the unit. I breathed a sigh of relief because I had found the problem, at least, one of them. Suddenly I felt the ship shake and I knew that it was not a good omen. I went to the quarterdeck and the gangway had already been pulled away from the ship. The large hausers that tie the ship to the pier were being cast off and the ship was getting underway.

As I watched the shoreline slowly disappearing, I thought to myself, "Why do these things happen to me?" Not knowing what else to do , I returned to Rang's stateroom. About two hours later, Rang did the same. When he had entered the stateroom, I asked him, "What is going on?" He replied, "There is a skirmish in the Digwar, Poonch area, the local authorities are badly outnumbered and five have been killed, the INS Gandhi has been ordered to sea to provide air support." I asked him, "Do you know who initiated the attack? He said,"It is probably the odious activity of Kashmiri separatist militants. There are two factions of them, the Lashkar-e-Tayyaba, "Army of the Righteous" and Jaish-e-Mohammad, "The Army of Mohammad", both are bad news." I then asked him a rather inane question, "Are there any Thugs still around?" He replied, " No, I have to think back in history a bit to answer that. The Thugs , from the Sanskrit sthag, "conceal or deceive" were a secret organization of robbers in India, who always strangled their victims. They were Devotees of the goddess Kali and would never strangle a woman. Due to "Thugee" activity against British soldiers and government officials, Lord William Bentinck, the British governor-general of India in 1829, investigated the Thug organization The campaign against the Thugs was directed by Sir W.H. Sleeman and was remarkably successful. Within seven years the Thugs were either imprisoned or hanged , and the organization was wiped out." I asked Rang, "Do you know how long we will be at sea?" He answered, "No, it will depend on how long it takes to us to quell the disturbance." I said, "Terrific!" He said, "It is time to eat and that we should go now." He led the way to the dining area that was the equivalent of the Officers Mess on United States ships.. Rang produced a chair for me and placed it next to him at the table that was his usual place. Most of the other Officers in the mess looked at me rather strangly, but did not say anything. Everyone waited until the Captain of the ship arrived and took his seat before the food was brought out. Some kind of warm tea seemed to be the beverage of the day. I wasn't sure what the food was, but it was fairly digestable, although I wished that the cooks would take it a little lighter on the curry. After the Captain had finished his meal and departed, the rest of the diners left also. I asked rang, "Is their someplace that I can buy some toiletries? He replied, "Yes there is a store on board." He led me to what would be called a "Ship's Store " on a U.S. Navel ship. This one was called a name that I could neither read or pronounce, any way, after standing in line for awhile, I was able to purchase a tooth brush; tooth paste, razor, shaving cream and some soap. Equipped with my toilet articles, we returned to Rang's stateroom. After I had stored my articles, I told Rang "I think that I have found the problem with the MoronUT18." Rang replied, "that is good news, do you think that you can repair it?" I told him, "I think that it can be fixed very easily if what I found is the only problem with the test equipment" He replied, "Excellent, we will address the problem tomorrow." Rang then suggested that we go watch flight operations. We then proceeded to an outside deck on the 08 level, the eighth deck above the main deck. By this time, the ship had passed Sri Lanka and was well on the way to it's station in the Arabian sea.

The Gandi had an armada of six Talwar Class Frigates and two Shtil Missile Launching Air Defense Ships encircling the Gandhi, forming a screen to protect the ship. On the rear of the flight deck, FRSMK-51 Sea Hairriers were leaving the flight deck vertically and then banking to the rear and then start their ascent to cruising altitude. Modified Rafale D. multi-role aircraft and modified Mig 25 Foxbats, India's fastest aircraft, were being connected to the catapults, where with a loud swish and a deafening roar, they were launched into the air. Even from where we were standing, we wished that we had some ear protection, as was worn by all the flight deck crew. The aircraft left the ship with fire blazing out of their jet pipes. They gained altitude very rapidly and soon faded into a dot on the horizon and finally disappeared all together. Above the ship and flying slightly to aft and to port, rear and left to land lubbers, escorting the ship was a SU-27SK Radar Aircraft. Rang told me, "The radar on this aircraft can search, detect and track up to ten targets with automatic assessment and prioritization." I asked Rang, "How difficult was it to modify aircraft that are used on land to aircraft duty." He replied, "We had to redesign the aircraft somewhat and we blew a lot of tires before we obtained stronger ones to stand the force of landing on an aircraft carrier."

The next morning, after a quick breakfast, we proceeded to the hanger deck to scrutinize the test equipment and determine how to get it in working order. Lok was summoned to the work area. I said to Rang, "Tell him that the equipment needs to be located in another area, because there was too many pieces of equipment connected to the power line that the MoronUT18 is connected to and that the electricity is too low for the machine to operate." After a rather lengthy discussion, none of which I understood, Rang told me "Lok tells me that this is the best place to bring aircraft in and out for testing and he doesn't want to move the machine." I told him, "Then a new power line will have to be run to connect the equipment to." After another lengthy conversation between Rang and Lok, Rang informed me "An electrician was being called to the work site. A crewman named Ganesh Chaturthi, probably the equivalent of a Chief Petty Officer in the U.S. Navy, arrived in the area. He was of medium height with a rounded face and very white teeth and of course, jet black hair. I told Rang, "Tell him that a new electrical power line needs to be run to the outlet where the test equipment is connected."

Rang passed the information along to Ganesh who then turned to me, and in fairly respectable English, asked me "Why you want to do this? " I repeated to him what I had told Rang and Lok. Ganesh then replied, "I can do this." He then went to a nearby telephone and made a call. Soon several crew members arrived and after receiving instructions from Ganesh, the crew started tracing out the electric line that powered the MoronUT18. After about a forty minute wait, Ganesh returned to the area and summoned me to come with him. He led me to a electric power distribution box one deck below the hanger deck. He pointed to a breaker that was connected to the cable that they had traced and then to an empty breaker in the same distribution box. Using my small multimeter, I checked the voltage on the spare breaker. It read 220 volts. I said to Ganesh, "This should work fine." He smiled and then turned to the other electrical workers and gave instructions to them.

I returned to the hanger deck and told Rang what was happening. He suggested, "Let us go have a meal while we wait," which we did. After we had eaten, we returned to the work site on the hangar deck. The electricians had brought the new power cable up from the deck below and were connecting it to the outlet which powered the Moron UT18. They had disconnected the old power cable from the outlet and the next power outlet in line that it was connected to. When they were finished, I turned to Lok and said, "You can test the machine now." The equipment was connected to an aircraft and the unit was turned on. The status board lighted up bright and clear. I could not read the writing on the status board, but Lok seemed happy with it. He turned to me smiled and held out his hand. I shook it and breathed a sigh of relief, apparently the unit was working as it was supposed to now.

The next four days were fairly uneventful. I spent most days watching flight operations. The flight deck reminded me of a beehive, small tractors were pulling aircraft to and from the hangar deck, moving in all different directions, somehow everything managed to get where it was supposed to be. I would look out at the dark blue sea at the white tipped waves dancing around the ship. There were ever present gulls following the ship looking for a hand-out and I would see an occasional shark. The nights were pretty quiet except for two nights when they held night flight operations. Every time that they fired one of the catapults, there was a loud Ka-Whoosh and my body would spring about three inches off the mattress.

Finally, on the morning of sixth day, Rang told me that we were going back to the Vizag Dockyard. By that time my khakis were taking on a color of their own and I was glad that I would be getting out of them. Later that evening, I changed into my suit and threw the khakis into a trash can. I then proceeded to the Flight Deck and watched the shoreline slowly appear. Tug boats came to meet the ship and pushed it slowly to the pier where it would dock. I watched the turbulent water that roiled up from the slowly turning of the ships screws. At last, the ship was pushed into the pier and the mooring lines were cast out and fastened to bollards by workers on the pier.

I met Rang at the Quarterdeck, where the gangway,

stairs to the pier, had been installed. We said our good-byes and I thanked him for his hospitality while I was on the ship. He thanked me for getting the test equipment operational and then returned to his shipboard duties. I turned to the Officer-of-the-Deck and asked "Permission to leave the ship sir", he gave me a quizzical look then smiled and waved as I departed the ship. I walked down to the gate where I had left Rajah and wondered where he was today. I managed to flag another taxi, and with much gesturing and slow enunciation, I told him that I wanted to go to the Ramada Hotel at Juhu Beach in Mumbai. He nodded affirmative when he heard me say "Juhu Beach." After a lengthy negotiation, we settled on the price of the fare, which was somewhat more than Rajah would charge me. It took about all the rupees that I had left. I settled into the taxi for the ride back to Mumbai.

As the taxi moved along with the traffic, I looked out the window at the countryside, I observed that India is a highly populated land with many diverse cultures. I would think that it would be hard to know what customs to observe and not to observe as a person travels from area to area. I would not want to live here, but I had enjoyed being away from the office, I thought of the ubiquitous bickering, back stabbing and onerous tasks that would be assigned to me after I got back to the facility. After a drive that took three and one half hours we arrived at the hotel. I paid the driver the sum that we had agreed upon and then entered the hotel.

When I went to the service desk, the same clerk that I had spoken to when I checked in came to meet me with a big smile on his face. "Where have you been?", He asked,

"I have some good news for you Mr. Stinson" he said, " We have been keeping your room for you and your luggage has arrived, it is in your room."   I thought to myself, "Terrific" and thanked the clerk for the information and then, with a bell hop in tow, or whatever they are called in India, I went on to my room to retrieve my luggage. With the bell hop carrying my luggage, I returned to the service desk and paid my bill with a VISA Government Credit Card.  I knew that I would catch flack from the Disbursing Office because of the amount of the bill, but I really didn't care.

I exchanged some more American dollars into rupees, with my accompanying bell hop, I departed the hotel and motioned for one of the taxis waiting outside.  I tipped the bell hop four American dollars and entered the taxi for my trip to the airport.  When the taxi arrived at the airport. I paid my fare and went inside the airport to the ticket counter.  I was able to catch a flight to the United States five hours later.  The airplane arrived Sacramento at ten thirty at night, making it necessary for me to spend the night at the same hotel that I had stayed before.  The next day, I managed to catch a flight to the Dallas Ft. Worth Airport, where I had a three hour layover and then I caught a flight for my home destination.

I needed some rest, so I took two days off before reporting to work.  When I arrived at the office and made my report, the bosses were all smiles and congratulated me on a job well done.  That was the first time that that had happened.

Two weeks later there was a company wide meeting. Zeke Humbolt was awarded a commendation for averting a possible diplomatic crisis with a foreign country.

# CHAPTER 11

Zeke Humbolt called Bid Brashear into his office. He told Bid that, "We have been directed to select and purchase a new Flight Analyzer for one of our Contract Aircraft, who do you think that we should assign the project to?" "Stinson", Bid replied. Zeke declared, "I don't like Stinson, can't you put someone else on the project?" Bid told him that'" In order to purchase new equipment, we have to do a Feasibility Study and an Economic Analysis, Stinson is the only one that has had the training to do that." Reluctantly, Zeke said, "Put him on it right away."

After their conversation, Bid told his Secretary "Have Stinson come to my office as soon as possible." Bid's secretary then called and relayed the message to me. I arrived at Bid's Office, knocked on his door and went in. Bid told me, "Sit down, I have an important project for you." He then explained the project that had been directed to the Equipment Project Office and what role I was to play in the project. He then told me that "You are to spend all of your time and energy on this project." He asked me, "If I had any questions?" I said, "Just one, do I have a free hand in accomplishing this project?" "Yes, now get on it", was his reply.

The Feasibility Study and Economic Analysis were long and tedious processes and took me two weeks to complete. After I was finished, they were looked at very little. The final results were favorable, but I could have skewed the reports in any direction that I wanted to. I then started contacting various companies that might have the type of equipment that I was looking for. I was told by one Company Agent that " We are currently testing a new Flight Analyzer at a Military Complex near Canton, Ohio." I reported this finding to Bid, who told me, " Make arrangements to go there and see what they have to offer." He then told me, "Include Darrel Studebaker, an Aircraft Equipment Specialist, in your arrangements." I asked him, "Why Studebaker?" Bid replied, "I want someone who is knowledgeable to look at the device." I said , "I will get started right away." I left his office with deep feelings of misgivings.

When the time came to travel, Darrel's wife drove us to the airport. When Darrel was through declaring his " Undying love" to his wife, we entered the airport terminal, boarded our aircraft and were off to Canton, Ohio.

After arriving at the Airport Terminal, I rented a car and we departed to a Madison Hotel and checked in. We then drove to the Mililtary Complex. When we arrived at the Complex,, we showed our identification and orders to a smartly dressed Gate Guard who directed us to Building 17B.

We drove to Building 17B, parked the car and entered the building. We were met by a Lieutenant who was very cordial and professional. He took us to a Colonel Hebner's Office and introduced us. Colonel Hebner was a distinguished looking gentleman with gray hair and bushy eyebrows to match. He was dressed in a green uniform with a large arrangement of ribbons on his chest. We told the Colonel what our mission was. He welcomed us and told us, " If I can do anything to help you while you are here, let me know." He said that , "Tomorrow morning would be a good time to be at hangar 5, as there would be some test flights at that time." We thanked the Colonel and departed and drove back to the hotel.

That evening we had dinner and the visited one of the local Night Clubs. It was nice to relax for awhile and unwind. Around eleven o'clock, Darrel disappeared for about a half hour. When he returned, he said" I need the keys to the car, I think I'm in love." Standing a few feet behind him was one of the ugliest women that I have ever seen. I asked him," How am I supposed to get back to the hotel?" He said, "Take a cab." I exclaimed, "Swell" and tossed him the keys. He then happily departed with his new "True Love".

The next morning I banged on Darrel's door at 6:00 AM. He mumbled, Go away!" I yelled back, " Come on get up, we have to be at the hanger by 7:00." He finally dragged himself to the door and opened it. His eyes looked like two red striped marbles with holes in them. With my encouragement, he got dressed and we departed for the Military Complex.

We arrived at Hanger 5 on time and met with some

Test Pilots, Ground Crew and a Factory Representative. When we had been there a few minutes, Darrel said," I have to do some research." He then found a comfortable chair, opened his laptop computer and promptly went to sleep.

One of the Test Pilots asked me, " Would you like to go on a test flight?" I answered eagerly, " I surely would." I was furnished some flight gear and we climbed into the aircraft. The pilot taxied out onto the tarmac to wait for permission to take off. Permission was given and I was taken for the most exhilarating ride that I have ever had in my life. The test flight was also a practice strafing run. The pilot completely obliterated the targets with rockets and thirty millimeter projectiles. He then put the aircraft through every maneuver imaginable. My stomach began to feel queasy and I was glad that I had not eaten breakfast. The pilot brought the aircraft in for a landing and taxied to a stop.

On somewhat shaky legs, I disembarked from the aircraft. I asked the pilot, "What is your opinion of the Flight Analyzer that is being tested?" He replied, "So far, it seems to be okay and is superior to what we have had before." I talked to the Factory Representative for awhile and he gave me some printed information on the equipment. I thanked everyone for their courtesy, I woke Darrel up and then we departed for the hotel to check out and then proceeded to the airport to return the rental car and catch our flight back to our home destination.

My next trip was to a National Guard Unit near Baltimore, Maryland, where Another company's Flight Analyzer was being tested. This time I had more than enough company on the trip. Besides Darrel Studebaker, there was: a Test Pilot named Bob Bundy, a lab Technician whose name was Alex Cardenas and Zeke Humbolt. I asked Darrel," Why is Zeke coming along?" Darrel confided," Officially he is going to oversee the project, unofficially, he has a girl friend in Baltimore."

The gang of five met at the airport and we boarded the aircraft for the flight to Baltimore. After we landed, Zeke rented a mini-van and we departed to a Ramada Inn that was ten miles from nowhere. Zeke said, "It is too late to do anything at the national Guard Unit today" and then he left in the Mini-van.

That evening Alex, who was of Spanish descent, five feet nine inches tall thick black hair and a small scar on his face , and I strolled around the neighborhood. The only businesses there were a small Grocery Store and two sleazy bars. We confirmed our suspicion that it wasn't worth the effort to stroll around the neighborhood.

The next morning we ate breakfast in the Hotel Resturant and then departed to the National Guard Unit. We met with some of the Test Pilots, Ground Crew members and the Factory Representative. I had a good conversation with one of the Test Pilots. I asked him, "What is your opinion of the Flight Analyzer that is being tested here?" He replied, "It is pretty good most of the time, but it is difficult to position just right." He confided,"I would take you for a test flight, but there are too many in your party.", I agreed with him.

I then talked to the factory Representative. We discussed various aspects of the equipment and he gave me some Company Brochures that had information about the Flight Analyzer. I then talked to a Supply Sergeant, who was going to take me to see some peripheral equipment.

Before we could leave, Zeke said, "OK lets go, we have done all that we can here." "I told Zeke that I would like some more time to get some more information." He replied, "If you want a ride to the hotel, you will come with us now!" We all piled into the Mini-van and Zeke drove back to the hotel, dropped us off and went on his not so secret mission. Alex exclaimed," At least we are back in time for lunch."

After dinner that evening, the rest of the crew ventured out to survey the populace of the local Gin Mills. I went to the hotel bar and got smashed. I awoke with an Excedrin headache, wondering just where I was.

At nine o'clock, everyone managed to meet in the hotel lobby, check out and pile into the Mini-van for our trip to the Airport Terminal. When we arrived at the Airport Terminal, Zeke turned the rental vehicle in and then the red-eyed gang of five boarded the aircraft for our flight home. As the aircraft taxied down the runway, my head was pounding from my excess drinking the night before. When the aircraft's wheels had lifted off of the pavement and the aircraft began it's ascent, I wondered, " why I had even been included in this trip."

My enthusiasm for this project was beginning to wane considerably. Too many people were getting involved to complete the kind of investigation that needed to be done. To keep my sanity, I made the recommendation that we purchase the Flight Analyzer that we looked at in the Military Complex in Canton, Ohio. Everyone agreed and a purchase order was submitted for approval. The purchase order was quickly approved and we received the Flight Analyzer in two weeks. The Factory Representative came to the Repair Facility to demonstrate the operation of the equipment and answer any questions that anyone had. Everyone seemed happy with the equipment and they started using it on a regular basis.

A few weeks later the CEO held an ALL Employees Meeting. At the meeting there was an Awards Ceremony. One of the employees who received an award was Darrel Studebaker. He received a commendation and a five hundred dollar award for his outstanding work in selecting and purchasing a new Flight Analyzer, which detects errors and makes the aircraft safer for the pilots and crew. After the meeting, I returned to my desk, sat down and hovered over it, reminiscent of the Industrial Revolution.